# MARK ANTHONY BROWN

# THE DRAGON'S EGG

Copyright @ Mark Anthony Brown 2024
Mark Anthony Brown asserts the moral right to be identified as the author of this work

All Rights Reserved.
This novel is entirely a work of fiction.
The names, characters and incidents portrayed in it are the work of the author's imagination. Any resemblance to actual persons, living or dead, events or localities is entirely coincidental.

All rights reserved. No part of this publication may be reproduced, stored in a retrieval system, or transmitted, in any form or by any means, electronic, mechanical, photocopying, recording or otherwise, without the prior permission of the publisher.

# Prologue

In a valley hidden from the eyes of the world, between two great mountains where the clouds hung low and soft like a veil, there was a village called Qingyun. To the outside world, it was a place of no great importance - just a quiet little village nestled among lush rice fields and sprawling orchards, where life moved with the seasons, and the people were content with their simple lives.

But there was a secret, one older than the village itself, a secret whispered through the generations, passed down by the elders around fireside tales. It was the story of the dragons.

Long ago, dragons roamed the world freely, their scales shimmering like the sun, their wings as wide as the sky. These creatures, full of ancient wisdom, were the keepers of magic. It was said that whenever a dragon appeared, magic would return to the world - gifts of prosperity, healing, and wisdom would follow in its wake. The seasons would change with gentle predictability, crops would grow in abundance, and the land itself would come alive with magic. But as quickly as they came, the dragons vanished, leaving only whispers behind them.

The people of Qingyun believed that one day, a dragon would return, and when it did, they must protect it. They did not know how, or when, but the villagers knew that the dragons were not to be controlled or captured. They were meant to be free, to bring balance to the world.

And so, they waited.

Little did they know, the dragon would not appear as the legends foretold. It would come in the form of an egg, hidden in the earth, waiting for the right person to find it. That person was a curious, brave boy named Li Wei - and the dragon's return would change the fate of Qingyun forever.

## CHAPTER ONE

# The Egg in the Orchard

The village of Qingyun sat quietly in the heart of a misty valley, the kind of place where the air always seemed to hold a soft whisper, as though the mountains themselves were telling secrets. The villagers had always known this valley to be a place of peace and plenty - rich fields of rice, orchards heavy with fruit, and rivers that sparkled with the kind of clarity one could only find in stories. Life was simple in Qingyun, and the people there, humble and hardworking, lived off the land with joy in their hearts.

And then there was Li Wei.

At twelve years old, Li Wei had the sort of mind that wandered when others were busy. While his friends worked in the fields, bending their backs to tend the crops, Li Wei could often be found sitting at the edge of the orchard, gazing up at the sky, his thoughts drifting like the clouds above him. He was the kind of boy who felt a strange pull in the air when the wind whispered through the trees, as if the world was waiting for something. He often imagined that somewhere, just beyond the misty hills, magic existed - waiting to be discovered.

His father, Li Jin, was a farmer who tended to the rice paddies, while his mother, Mei, worked in the orchard, caring for the fruit trees. Li Wei loved the village with all his heart, but he often wondered if there might be more to life than tending crops and harvesting fruit. More than once, he had heard his grandmother, Grandmother Xiu, speak of ancient legends - of dragons that brought magic to the world. The idea of magic enchanted him more than anything else, though he kept these thoughts mostly to himself. He knew, as most of the villagers did, that life in Qingyun was blessed, but magic seemed far away, like the stars that blinked above at night.

One afternoon, while playing near a hidden grove in the orchard, Li Wei wandered further than usual. The grove, a quiet corner of the orchard where the trees grew thick and tangled, was his favourite place to escape to when the world felt too noisy. Today, however, it was different. The sunlight, usually soft and dappled through the branches, seemed to shimmer strangely on the ground.

There, half-buried in the earth beneath an old peach tree, was something that caught Li Wei's eye - a large, smooth egg that glowed faintly in the dim light. He crouched down and gently brushed away the dirt around it. The egg was unlike anything he had ever seen before, its surface shimmered with a strange iridescent glow, as if the light of the sun was trapped inside, refracting into colours he had no name for.

The air around it felt warmer than the rest of the grove, and the egg pulsed, as if it were alive.

'Is it... a treasure?' Li Wei whispered to himself, his heart racing with excitement. He had read about treasures hidden in the earth, about rare jewels and forgotten relics. But this... this felt different.

With careful hands, he lifted the egg, marvelling at how warm it felt. It seemed impossibly light for its size, and as he cradled it against his chest, he could almost hear a soft hum, like a heartbeat. It was unlike any treasure he'd ever imagined - and more than anything, it felt like something important, something that needed to be protected.

'I'll take you home,' Li Wei murmured to the egg, though he didn't expect it to answer. He tucked it into the folds of his shirt and hurried back toward the village, his mind spinning with possibilities. What could it be? And more importantly, what should he do with it?

***

Back at the small, tidy house where Li Wei lived with his family, he carefully placed the egg in a soft cloth on the table in the corner of the kitchen. His mother, Mei, was busy preparing dinner, and his father, Li Jin, was outside sharpening his tools.

Li Wei decided not to tell them just yet. It was too strange, too mysterious. They might dismiss it as a curiosity or an oddity. But Li Wei knew, deep down, that the egg was special. It called to him, and something in his heart told him that it was not an ordinary find.

Over the next few days, Li Wei kept the egg in the corner of his room, tending to it as though it were a fragile plant. He wrapped it in the softest cloths, making sure it was kept warm and safe. Every now and then, he would sneak peeks at it, wondering if it would reveal its secret.

Then, on the fourth day, as Li Wei sat by the window, watching the clouds roll by, he heard a sound - soft, like a crackling of wood. He turned, startled, and saw that the egg had begun to crack. Small fissures appeared along its smooth surface, like spider webs spreading across glass. A warm, golden light poured through the cracks, illuminating the room with an almost blinding glow.

Li Wei's heart raced as he leaned forward, eyes wide. The cracks widened further, and then - *pop!* - the top of the egg broke away with a soft sound, revealing a small creature inside.

It was a *dragon*.

The tiny dragon looked up at Li Wei with wide, curious eyes, its scales gleaming like polished gold. It was no bigger than a kitten, its wings still tiny and folded against its back. The air around it seemed to shimmer with warmth and magic, and for a moment, Li Wei could hardly believe his eyes.

'Hello,' he whispered, his voice trembling with awe.

The dragon blinked, then stretched its tiny wings. With a soft, almost musical chirp, it crawled out of the broken egg, its little claws tapping lightly against the cloth. The warmth it emitted filled the room, like the glow of a distant star.

Li Wei smiled, a rush of joy and wonder flooding through him. 'I'll call you *Longzi*,' he said, his voice full of affection. 'Little Dragon.'

The dragon tilted its head, as if it understood. Then, as if to prove the connection between them, it let out a small burst of flame - no bigger than the flicker of a candle - and the flame danced in the air before disappearing. Li Wei laughed in delight.

It was then that he realised, this was not just an ordinary creature. It was something magical - something he had always dreamed of. And perhaps, just perhaps, magic was real after all.

But for now, Li Wei kept *Longzi* a secret. He didn't know yet what kind of magic this dragon might bring into the world, but he could feel deep in his heart that it was something extraordinary.

And so, with the little dragon curled up on his bed that night, Li Wei drifted into a dreamless sleep, knowing that life in Qingyun - his quiet, peaceful village - was about to change forever.

## CHAPTER TWO

# The Magic of Longzi

The days following Longzi's hatching passed in a blur of wonder. Li Wei had never imagined that a creature so small, so delicate, could have such an impact on the world around him. But the signs were clear. The fields were changing.

At first, it was subtle - a ripple in the air, a faint shimmer at the edges of the rice paddies. Then, within the span of a few days, the changes became undeniable. The rice plants, once slender and green, now grew thick and golden, bending under the weight of the largest grains anyone in Qingyun had ever seen. The orchard, which had always yielded fruit in abundance, began to produce fruit so sweet and plump that it seemed almost too perfect to be real. The apples were as red as rubies, the peaches gleamed like polished copper, and the grapes burst from their vines, glistening in the sunlight.

Li Wei couldn't help but notice the quiet magic that surrounded Longzi. The dragon, though still small enough to fit into the palm of his hand, seemed to radiate warmth and light wherever it went. At dawn, when Li Wei would visit the fields, Longzi would stretch its wings and flutter about, chasing the soft morning light. The crops would sway with the breeze, as though reaching for the dragon's presence.

One evening, as the sun dipped below the horizon and the last tendrils of daylight turned the sky a soft shade of rose, Li Wei stood on the hill overlooking the village. Longzi was perched on his shoulder, its golden scales sparkling faintly in the dimming light. Together, they watched the village below - a village that seemed to be glowing with life, prosperity, and energy.

Li Wei felt a deep sense of peace, but also something more - a powerful connection to the land and the creatures around him. He knew that this magic, this change, was no accident. It was Longzi, the little dragon who had come from the mysterious egg. And as much as he had come to love Longzi, Li Wei also began to wonder what this magic would mean for him - and for everyone in the village.

The next day, as the villagers gathered in the square for their usual market, the atmosphere was brighter than ever before. People were laughing, exchanging goods, and trading stories. Even the air itself seemed lighter, the scent of the harvest sweeter.

Li Wei's mother, Mei, smiled as she picked up a basket of plump peaches and handed it to the elderly widow who lived at the edge of the village. 'Take some,' Mei said, her voice soft with kindness. 'The harvest is bountiful this year.'

The widow's wrinkled face lit up with gratitude. 'I've never seen fruit like this in all my days,' she said, pressing the peaches to her chest as if they were treasures. 'Something is happening in Qingyun. It's as if the earth herself is blessing us.'

Li Wei stood a little further back, observing the scene. Longzi, ever the curious creature, fluttered from person to person, chirping happily. The villagers had long since grown accustomed to the little dragon's presence, and it was clear that the magic had only brought them closer together. People smiled brighter, shared more freely, and felt a renewed sense of hope and joy.

Later that evening, as the moon rose high in the sky, the children of Qingyun gathered by the great oak tree in the village square. *Elder Lin*, the oldest and wisest of the villagers, was there, as she often was, her silver hair gleaming in the moonlight. Her sharp eyes twinkled as she addressed the children, who were all excited to hear the next of her stories.

'Tonight,' Elder Lin said in her soft, steady voice, 'I will tell you of the dragons - the ancient creatures who brought magic into the world.'

The children leaned in, eager to hear. Li Wei, of course, was listening closely, his heart thudding with excitement. He already knew something about the dragon's magic, but Elder Lin's words held a weight of ancient knowledge he longed to understand.

Elder Lin began, her voice carrying the wisdom of many years.

'Long ago, before even the first rice was planted, dragons roamed the earth. They were the *keepers of magic*, the guardians of the world's prosperity. The people of the land, simple and wise, revered them as beings of great power and grace. And the dragons - like Longzi here - brought with them blessings, bountiful harvests, clear skies, and peace.'

The children gasped, their eyes wide as they pictured the magnificent creatures in their minds. But Elder Lin's gaze grew more serious.

'But,' she continued, her voice lowering, 'there is an old warning that goes with the coming of dragons. For with magic comes *danger*. Dragons are not meant to be controlled, for their power is ancient and unpredictable. And so, evil men have always sought them - greedy kings, dark sorcerers, and warlords who would try to use the dragons' power for their own gain. We must always protect them, for if a dragon is captured or harmed, the magic it carries can turn… *dark*.'

Li Wei felt a shiver run down his spine at the thought. The villagers, too, were silent, considering Elder Lin's words. The peace they had enjoyed for so long might be fragile, after all.

'You must remember,' Elder Lin said, looking at the children with a grave expression, 'dragons are not to be treated lightly. They are precious. And if you are ever blessed to have one in your life - like Li Wei with Longzi - you must protect them, just as they protect you.'

Li Wei's heart thudded in his chest. He looked down at Longzi, who was perched happily on his shoulder, watching the world with its bright, intelligent eyes. The little dragon chirped a soft sound, as though acknowledging the weight of the old legend.

***

As the days passed, Li Wei's connection with Longzi deepened. The dragon had grown quickly - its wings now strong enough to carry it through the air for short bursts, its scales gleaming like molten gold. Longzi would often follow Li Wei around the village, leaping from tree to tree, fluttering down to rest at Li Wei's feet when he sat by the river, or curling up at the foot of his bed when night fell.

It was not just the village that had changed. Li Wei had changed, too.

The more time he spent with Longzi, the more he felt an odd clarity, as though his mind had been sharpened, his thoughts clearer. He found himself solving problems with ease, understanding things that once seemed difficult. In the evenings, he would sit with his mother, helping her plan their next harvest, and his insights would amaze her. It wasn't just knowledge he had learned - it was something deeper, something wiser, as though the magic in Longzi had somehow awakened a part of him, too.

At times, he would find himself thinking, *Is this what magic feels like?*

Longzi would look at him then, as if understanding, and chirp softly, its golden eyes twinkling with mischief and mystery.

Together, they were a team - inseparable, bound by a magic neither of them fully understood yet.

But as the village continued to flourish, and as Li Wei's own abilities grew sharper with each passing day, one thing became clear, Longzi was not just a dragon. He was a force - something ancient and powerful, with the ability to change everything around them.

And though Li Wei didn't know it yet, the greatest test of their friendship - and the village's prosperity - was still to come.

## CHAPTER THREE

# The Threat of Lord Xian

The village of Qingyun had always been a place of quiet harmony, where every sunrise brought hope and every sunset brought peace. But the winds of change were stirring, and with them came a shadow that no one had expected.

It began, as such things often do, with whispers - quiet rumours carried on the breeze from faraway lands. At first, the villagers paid little attention. But as the days passed, the whispers grew louder, until they could no longer be ignored.

It was said that in a kingdom far to the north, there lived a lord - a man with eyes as cold as stone, and a heart as black as midnight. *Lord Xian* was a warlord, cruel and ambitious, who sought nothing more than to dominate all the lands. But more than land or gold, Lord Xian hungered for *power* - the kind of power that could make him immortal, the kind of power that could never be taken from him.

And in the secret, whispered corners of his castle, Lord Xian had heard of a way to achieve such power. A dragon.

For dragons were not mere beasts of legend. They were the keepers of magic, the ancient creatures that held the balance of the world in their wings. And it was said that whoever controlled a dragon would hold dominion over all things - nature, time, and life itself.

Lord Xian had heard the rumours of a dragon born in the quiet village of Qingyun. And as the stories of the village's newfound prosperity spread - of crops that grew heavy with harvest, of fruit that gleamed like jewels - he knew that the dragon must be the source. Longzi, the little dragon who had brought such blessings, was no longer a secret.

In the cold, dark chambers of his castle, Lord Xian's mind began to hatch a plan - one that would see him become the most powerful man the world had ever known.

*\*\*\**

Meanwhile, in Qingyun, life seemed as usual. The harvest was in full swing, the villagers working side by side, laughing and singing as they reaped the fruits of their labour. Li Wei, more content than he had ever been, spent his days by Longzi's side, feeling the dragon's warmth and watching as the creature grew stronger with each passing day. Together, they wandered the fields, basking in the magic that flowed through the earth.

But one evening, a strange group of travellers arrived in Qingyun - four men with cloaks of fine black cloth, their faces hidden beneath wide-brimmed hats. They were traders, they claimed, from a distant province, come to exchange rare goods with the villagers. At first glance, they seemed harmless enough, but something about them made Li Wei uneasy. Their eyes were too sharp, their smiles too quick. And whenever they looked at Longzi, their gaze lingered just a moment too long.

Over the course of several days, the strangers grew more familiar, speaking with the villagers, offering their goods for trade, and asking curious questions. They were particularly interested in the harvest, commenting on the way the crops had grown in such abundance. They were polite, always gracious, but there was a certain coldness in their manners that made Li Wei's stomach twist.

It wasn't long before the truth dawned on him. These men were not traders at all. They were spies - sent by Lord Xian, no doubt, to learn more about Longzi and the dragon's magic.

Li Wei shared his suspicions with his parents, but they dismissed them with a shake of the head. 'You're imagining things,' his father, Li Jin, said with a smile. 'Not everyone who visits Qingyun is a threat, Wei. We mustn't become paranoid.'

But Li Wei couldn't shake the feeling that something was terribly wrong. He watched Longzi more closely than ever, his heart heavy with worry. The dragon, for all its joy and playfulness, had grown larger and stronger, its golden scales gleaming in the sunlight, its wings fluttering with energy. The village had prospered in ways no one could have predicted. But Li Wei knew that magic of such magnitude could not go unnoticed. He only hoped it wasn't too late.

\*\*\*

One moonless night, when the village lay cloaked in darkness, the soldiers came.

At first, there was nothing more than a strange rustling at the edge of the village - a soft, distant sound that might have been the wind. But then came the footsteps. Quiet at first, then growing louder, until the unmistakable thud of boots on dirt echoed through the narrow streets.

Li Wei was awoken by the sound of his mother's urgent voice. 'Wei, get up. Now.'

His heart raced as he jumped from his bed and hurried to the window. What he saw made his blood run cold.

A dozen soldiers, clad in black armour, were silently marching toward the centre of the village. Their faces were hidden behind masks, their movements sharp and precise, like a pack of wolves closing in on their prey.

'Longzi,' Li Wei whispered, his voice barely a breath. The little dragon had been asleep at the foot of his bed, but now it stirred, its

## THE DRAGON'S EGG

golden eyes opening wide. Longzi chirped softly, sensing the danger, and flapped its wings nervously.

Before Li Wei could reach out to protect it, the door to his room burst open. His father stood in the doorway, his face pale and grim.

'Stay close to me, Wei,' he said, grabbing Li Wei's arm. 'They're after the dragon.'

Li Wei's heart dropped. The soldiers were not here for goods, nor were they here for trade. They were here for *Longzi*.

Outside, in the heart of the village, the soldiers had already reached the square. The dragon, sensing the danger, darted toward the trees, but it was too late. With swift, practiced movements, the soldiers surrounded Longzi, drawing nets and ropes to trap the creature.

'Get away from him!' Li Wei shouted, running out into the square, but his voice was drowned out by the clatter of armour and the shouts of the soldiers.

The soldiers, led by a tall man with a cruel, twisted smile, closed in on Longzi, who struggled to escape, its wings flapping wildly, but the ropes were too strong. The dragon's flame sputtered out in a puff of smoke, its magic momentarily stifled by the tight bonds.

Li Wei rushed forward, desperation flooding his every step. 'No! Stop!'

But it was too late. With a swift motion, the soldiers placed Longzi in a cage - a dark, iron contraption that held the dragon tightly, keeping it from moving. The creature let out a low, mournful cry, its golden eyes filled with confusion and fear.

'No!' Li Wei cried, falling to his knees in front of the cage. 'Please, don't take him.'

The tall soldier, his face obscured by a mask, stepped forward and sneered. 'The dragon belongs to Lord Xian now. His magic will make him more powerful than any king. The world will fall at his feet.'

'Lord Xian...' Li Wei whispered, his heart breaking as he realised the truth. The warlord's ambition had reached Qingyun, and with it, the safety of his village - and his beloved dragon - was slipping away.

But Li Wei would not give up. He couldn't. He would not allow Longzi to be taken, no matter the cost. Even if the path ahead was filled with danger, he would find a way to rescue his friend.

For *Longzi* was more than just a dragon. He was the heart of the village, the magic that had brought hope and prosperity. And Li Wei would stop at nothing to protect him.

## CHAPTER FOUR

# The Rescue and the Final Battle

The night was quiet when Li Wei, heart heavy with determination, stood on the edge of Qingyun village, staring into the dark woods that stretched before him. Behind him, the villagers had gathered to watch as he, Jin, and Shan prepared to leave. The villagers had offered their support, but only these three were brave enough to follow through on the perilous journey ahead.

Li Wei knew what he had to do. He had to rescue Longzi.

Though the dragon was now locked away in Lord Xian's castle - trapped in a cage as cold and unyielding as the heart of the evil lord himself - Li Wei couldn't bear to think of Longzi suffering. The magic that the dragon carried was too important to be stolen by such cruelty, and Li Wei would stop at nothing to bring his friend back.

'You'll need more than courage,' Jin said, adjusting the pouch of herbs she carried at her waist. The clever girl with the sparkling eyes was sharp as a knife, and though she often kept to herself, her wit and intellect were as sharp as any blade. 'You'll need a plan.'

'I have one,' Li Wei said, his voice steady despite the storm of worry and anger swirling inside him. 'We get in, we find Longzi, and we get out. But it won't be easy.'

Beside him, Shan stood in silence, his eyes dark and thoughtful. Shan had never spoken much, but his bravery was as clear as his silent resolve. He was a quiet boy, always watching, always learning, and his knowledge of the land's traps and paths would be invaluable in the dangerous journey ahead.

With one final glance at the village, Li Wei nodded. 'Let's go.'

***

The journey through the thick forest was far from easy. The trees seemed to stretch endlessly, their branches twisting like dark fingers, and the path was treacherous - full of hidden thorns and steep inclines. But Jin, quick with her clever ideas, found shortcuts through the thick underbrush, and Shan's knowledge of the land kept them safe from wild animals and hidden dangers.

As the days wore on, Li Wei could feel the weight of his mission pressing on him. Every step brought him closer to Lord Xian's castle, and the closer they came, the more his thoughts turned to Longzi. He could feel the dragon's presence in his heart - longing to be free, to feel the wind beneath his wings once more.

At night, when the firelight flickered low, Li Wei would close his eyes and remember the way Longzi's golden scales shimmered in the sunlight, how the little dragon had curled up beside him at night and let out soft, contented chirps. That was the image that drove him forward - the bond between them, the magic of their friendship. Nothing could break that bond.

***

After days of travel, they finally reached the towering stone walls of Lord Xian's castle. The sight of it made Li Wei's heart drop. The castle was enormous, an imposing fortress that seemed to loom over the land like a dark cloud. Its walls were thick and high, with iron gates that glistened in the pale moonlight. From atop the walls, guards patrolled, their eyes sharp and watchful.

'We'll have to be careful,' Jin whispered, her fingers tapping the map she'd drawn of the castle's layout. 'I think there's a way in through the west gate - there's a hidden tunnel there, but it's well-guarded. We'll need to outwit them.'

Shan didn't speak, but he gave a slight nod. His eyes were scanning the walls, already thinking about the traps that might lay ahead.

'We'll get in,' Li Wei said firmly, his resolve unshaken. 'We've come this far. We're not turning back.'

\*\*\*

It took hours, but they finally managed to slip inside the castle under the cover of night. They moved silently through the dark hallways, their hearts pounding in their chests. The air was thick with the smell of damp stone and burning torches. As they crept closer to the heart of the castle, Li Wei's heart quickened. They were getting closer to Longzi, closer to the dragon's cage. But they had to move swiftly.

Finally, they reached the chamber where Longzi was kept. The dragon was there, locked in a cage of iron, its golden scales dulled by the darkness. Longzi's eyes, usually bright with life, were dim, filled with sadness and confusion. The sight of the dragon in such a state tore at Li Wei's heart.

'Longzi,' Li Wei whispered, stepping forward. But the dragon didn't move, not at first.

The heavy door to the chamber creaked, and from the shadows emerged Lord Xian himself. His cold, cruel eyes gleamed as he stepped forward, his voice smooth and mocking.

'Did you really think you could take the dragon from me?' Lord Xian sneered. 'The power of a dragon is not meant to be free, boy.

It is meant to be controlled. Once I possess its magic, I will be immortal. I will rule all of the lands!'

Li Wei's heart clenched in fury. 'You don't understand,' he said, his voice shaking but resolute. 'Longzi isn't meant to be controlled. Dragons are meant to be free, to bring prosperity, to keep the balance of magic in the world. You can't steal that from him. You'll never understand.'

Lord Xian's face twisted with disdain. 'You're just a child. You think you can save him? You think your little bond with this creature means anything? Magic is power, and I will control it!'

The lord raised his hand, and at his command, the cage tightened, trapping Longzi even further. The dragon let out a soft, mournful cry, and Li Wei's heart twisted in anguish. He had to act, and fast.

'Longzi!' Li Wei called, his voice filled with raw emotion. 'You're not alone. We're here. You don't belong to him.'

In that moment, something shifted. Longzi's golden eyes locked with Li Wei's, and for the first time in days, the dragon stirred. The cage, once unyielding, began to glow with a fierce, bright light. Longzi's wings fluttered as the magic inside the dragon surged, breaking free from its restraints. The ground beneath their feet trembled as the dragon's power awakened.

With a mighty roar, Longzi's form began to grow. His scales shimmered brighter than the sun, and his wings stretched wide, filling the chamber with an overwhelming light. Lord Xian stumbled backward, fear flickering in his eyes.

'No!' Lord Xian shouted, his voice cracking. 'This cannot be!'

But it was too late.

With a burst of flame and light, Longzi broke free from his cage. The entire castle shook as the dragon's magic surged outward, the walls cracking under the force of his power. Longzi's roar was deafening, echoing through the halls as the soldiers scrambled in terror.

Li Wei, Jin, and Shan stood back, watching in awe as the dragon grew to his full, majestic size. Lord Xian's soldiers, once confident in their control, were now no match for Longzi's fury. The dragon's flames blazed, sending the soldiers fleeing in every direction.

With one final, powerful blast of magic, Longzi sent Lord Xian fleeing from the castle, his once-proud figure disappearing into the night.

***

The journey back to Qingyun was filled with joy and relief. The village greeted them with cheers, their eyes wide with wonder as they saw Longzi - now a mighty, majestic dragon - flying high above the village, its golden scales gleaming in the sunlight.

Li Wei smiled, his heart light with happiness. 'We did it. We brought him home.'

Longzi landed softly at the edge of the village, his wings folding gracefully as he lowered himself to the ground. He chirped happily and nuzzled Li Wei, his golden eyes filled with affection.

And as the villagers gathered around, their faces shining with gratitude and awe, Li Wei realised that the magic Longzi had brought to the village was not just in the crops, the weather, or the prosperity. The true magic was in the bond they shared, the friendship that had been tested by fire and had come through stronger than ever.

Longzi was free. And so, too, was the village of Qingyun.

## CHAPTER FIVE

# A New Beginning

The sun had barely risen over Qingyun, its golden rays stretching across the village like a warm blanket, gently waking the earth. The fields were full, heavy with the ripest rice, the orchards bursting with fruit so sweet it almost seemed enchanted. Flowers bloomed in a riot of colour, and the air was fragrant with the scent of freshly baked bread, carried on the breeze.

Life had returned to normal, but it was a different kind of normal now. The village, once simple and quiet, had become a place of hope, of magic. And at the heart of it all stood *Longzi* - the golden dragon who had brought not just prosperity, but a new sense of unity to the land.

Li Wei stood at the edge of the village, watching as Longzi soared above the rooftops, his golden wings gleaming like the sun itself. The dragon's roar was a sound of triumph now, not fear - a roar that filled the air with joy and warmth.

It had been several weeks since the defeat of Lord Xian, and since then, the village had flourished in ways the villagers had never imagined. The rice had never been so plentiful, the fruit trees had never borne such sweet harvests, and even the weather seemed to smile down on Qingyun, with gentle rains falling at just the right time and the sun shining warmly without becoming too harsh. The magic that Longzi brought had seeped into everything - the very soil beneath their feet, the air they breathed, the hearts they carried.

But it wasn't just the land that had been blessed. The people of Qingyun had changed, too. They were kinder, more generous with one another. They shared their bounty, not out of obligation, but out of a newfound spirit of community. There was laughter in the streets, and every corner of the village seemed filled with life, the kind of life that came from deep, unshakable happiness.

Li Wei watched it all with pride, but also with a quiet sense of awe. In a way, it seemed impossible. After everything - after the fear, the uncertainty, the darkness that had crept into their lives - there was now light. And it wasn't just the sunlight that bathed the fields, it was the magic of friendship, the strength of loyalty, and the courage that had brought them through the worst.

'Are you going to stand there all day?' Jin's voice broke through his thoughts, and Li Wei turned to find her walking toward him, a mischievous glint in her eye. 'The day's already started, you know. Don't want to miss all the fun.'

Li Wei smiled, shaking his head. 'I was just thinking about everything that's changed. It feels like we're living in a dream sometimes.'

Jin shrugged, adjusting the pack on her back. 'I think we've earned the dream. And, to be fair, you did most of the hard work.' She grinned, her usual sharpness softened by the warmth of the village's new peace.

Li Wei laughed. 'We all did. You, Shan, the villagers - everyone played a part. It wasn't just me.'

Jin raised an eyebrow. 'Fair enough. But you were the one who faced Lord Xian down, remember? I'm not sure many would have done that.'

Li Wei looked away, his gaze drifting back to Longzi, who now hovered above the village, his wings catching the light. 'I didn't do it alone,' Li Wei said softly. 'And besides, I wasn't afraid. Not after I realised something important. Magic isn't just about power - it's about heart.'

Jin's eyes widened, her usual scepticism replaced by something more thoughtful. 'Heart?'

Li Wei nodded, his voice steady. 'I think that's what Longzi taught me. Magic doesn't come from strength or control. It comes from kindness, from loyalty. It comes from the bond you share with the world around you.'

Before Jin could reply, Shan appeared beside them, his quiet presence always somehow grounding. He nodded toward the hill that rose just outside the village. 'We should go. Longzi's waiting.'

***

The climb up the hill was peaceful, the path shaded by ancient trees whose leaves whispered in the breeze. As they reached the summit, Li Wei stopped, taking in the view. From here, he could see all of Qingyun - its green fields stretching endlessly, its rooftops gleaming beneath the sun. The village was vibrant with life, and all of it, Li Wei knew, had been touched by magic.

Longzi was perched atop the hill, his golden scales shimmering, his great wings folding neatly at his sides. His eyes - those deep, wise eyes - locked with Li Wei's, and in that moment, Li Wei felt a surge of love and gratitude for the dragon.

'Do you ever wonder what comes next?' Li Wei asked, sitting down beside Longzi. Jin and Shan sat as well, their faces soft with contentment.

Longzi let out a gentle, rumbling chirp and curled his tail around them, a gesture of comfort, of protection. Li Wei smiled, leaning against the dragon's warm scales. 'I guess we'll find out together,' he said, watching as the sun dipped lower in the sky, casting a soft orange glow over the land.

The world was peaceful now. The magic that Longzi brought wasn't just a gift, it was a promise. The bond between Li Wei and the dragon was a living thing - something that would grow and change as they did, something that would keep the village safe and strong.

And though Li Wei couldn't know exactly what adventures lay ahead, he knew one thing for certain: as long as Longzi remained in Qingyun, the village would always know prosperity, peace, and the magic of a shared heart.

***

The sunset bathed the hill in golden light, and for a long time, they sat in silence, watching as the stars began to twinkle softly in the sky. The future was uncertain, but it was a future filled with hope, and that was enough.

For Li Wei had learned that no matter what came next, *the greatest magic of all was the power of friendship, of heart, and of home.*

And as Longzi's wings fluttered gently in the evening breeze, Li Wei knew that the adventure was far from over. There was a whole world to explore, and together, they would face whatever came next - with courage, with kindness, and with magic in their hearts.

## CHAPTER SIX

# The Dragon's Farewell

Years passed in Qingyun, and the village continued to thrive under the benevolent protection of Longzi. The dragon's golden wings shimmered as he soared through the sky each day, his flames lighting up the horizon at sunset. The people of Qingyun were prosperous, their harvests abundant, and their hearts full of warmth and gratitude.

But in the quiet moments, when the winds whispered through the trees and the stars twinkled like lanterns in the night sky, Li Wei could sense a change. Longzi had grown, not just in size, but in wisdom. The bond they shared had become stronger, but Li Wei could feel that the dragon's journey was not yet complete. A restlessness had settled in the mighty creature's heart, one that spoke of the world beyond the mountains, of lands and people who had yet to feel the touch of magic.

One evening, as the sun began to set, painting the sky in hues of fiery orange and soft lavender, Longzi landed gently beside Li Wei at the top of the hill. The dragon's scales glistened in the fading light, and his golden eyes shone with a quiet sadness, as though he had already made a decision, he was reluctant to voice.

'Longzi,' Li Wei said softly, his voice steady but filled with unspoken understanding. 'You are leaving, aren't you?'

The dragon lowered his head, nuzzling Li Wei's shoulder. The bond between them pulsed with a warmth, a reassurance that the bond they shared would not be broken by distance or time. Li Wei's heart twisted, for though he had known this day would come, he wasn't ready to let go.

*'I've brought magic to this village, Li Wei,'* Longzi's voice rang out in Li Wei's mind, clear and deep like the rumble of distant thunder. *'But there is more magic to spread. There are people who have yet to know the blessings of kindness, of prosperity, of harmony. The world beyond these mountains is waiting. It is time for me to go.'*

Li Wei's chest tightened, but he nodded, though the words caught in his throat. 'I understand. But... will you be alright? What will happen to Qingyun without you?'

The dragon's golden eyes softened, a light flickering in their depths. *'You are not alone, Li Wei. You have the heart of a true friend, the soul of a protector. That is what has made this village flourish, what has made it magic. It is time for you to take what I have given you and carry it forward.'*

With those words, Longzi reached out with his great tail, brushing it across Li Wei's hand. A burst of golden light surrounded them both, and Li Wei felt a warmth, a powerful surge of magic coursing through him. It was as if the dragon's very essence had entered him, filling him with strength, clarity, and wisdom. Longzi was giving him a gift - one more precious than any treasure, more powerful than any magic he had ever known.

'Longzi,' Li Wei whispered, his heart full. 'You're giving me your magic.'

Longzi's voice was filled with pride. *'Not just my magic, Li Wei. I'm giving you my trust. You have the power to protect the village, to ensure that the magic we have here continues. The world will change, and you will be the guardian of this place, just as I have been. But remember this - magic is not in the strength of your power. It is in the kindness of your heart. The world needs your heart more than ever.'*

Li Wei's mind raced as he absorbed Longzi's words. The weight of the responsibility was immense, but it was also a comfort. He knew, in the deepest part of himself, that he was ready.

'I will protect them,' Li Wei said, his voice steady with newfound confidence. 'I will protect Qingyun, and I will honour the magic you've given me.'

Longzi gave a soft, rumbling laugh that filled the air like the sound of distant thunder. *'I know you will, Li Wei. You have already proven your heart is true. You will continue to make this place prosper, and you will carry the magic with you wherever you go.'*

With one final, lingering touch of his tail, Longzi stood tall, his wings stretching wide, casting a shadow over the land. The wind rose around him, carrying the scent of distant lands, calling him to spread the magic he had awakened.

Li Wei stepped back, his heart heavy, but proud. 'Goodbye, my friend,' he whispered, the words almost lost in the wind.

Longzi paused for a moment, looking down at Li Wei with a gaze filled with warmth and affection. *'This is not a goodbye,'* the dragon's voice echoed in Li Wei's mind. *'I will always be with you - in the wind, in the sky, in the magic that will never leave you. Our bond is eternal.'*

With a mighty roar that shook the earth, Longzi spread his wings and soared into the sky, rising higher and higher until he was but a golden speck against the vast expanse of the heavens. The sun dipped below the horizon, and with it, the last golden trace of the dragon disappeared.

## CHAPTER SEVEN

# The Call Beyond the Mountains

The village of Qingyun was but a speck beneath Longzi's wings as he soared higher and higher into the sky, leaving the place that had been his home for so long. The golden dragon's wings beat steadily, creating powerful gusts of wind that made the trees below sway. Far beneath him, the village nestled in the valley, its rice fields swaying like a patchwork quilt, the people moving about their daily chores, unaware that the dragon who had brought them prosperity was now heading beyond the mountains, toward lands unknown.

Longzi's heart fluttered in his chest - both heavy with the sadness of leaving and light with the excitement of the adventure ahead. He had long known that his journey was far from over. Magic, after all, was meant to be spread across the world, and he had felt its call, a whisper that tugged at his very soul. He had learned much in Qingyun, but now the world awaited him, vast and full of mysteries he had yet to uncover.

The wind ruffled his golden scales, catching the sunlight and scattering it into a thousand sparkles. Longzi looked back one last time, watching the sun dip behind the distant mountains, painting the sky in shades of orange and pink. He could almost feel the heartbeat of the land beneath him, and for a brief moment, he wondered if he had made the right choice.

But then the call came.

It wasn't like anything he had ever heard before. It wasn't a voice, exactly, but a *feeling*, a pull deep in his chest that seemed to come from the very heart of the earth. It was as though something inside him was reaching out, beckoning him. It was soft at first, a gentle tug on his heartstrings, but soon it grew stronger, more insistent, until Longzi could no longer ignore it.

*A dragon?* he thought. Could it be another dragon calling to him, as he had once called to the skies, yearning for companionship, for understanding? For a fleeting moment, Longzi felt the comforting sensation of belonging, the hope that he might finally find another of his kind, someone who could share the magic that had shaped his life.

But even as the thought bloomed in his mind, something in the air began to shift. The winds turned colder, the sky darker, and a strange shiver ran down Longzi's spine. The call was sharp, distant yet deep, like a melody played on a broken instrument - its tone both alluring and dangerous.

Longzi hesitated in midair, his wings momentarily faltering. What was this? The call was now louder, vibrating through his body, like a pulse that throbbed in time with his heart. Something was pulling him toward it, something *wrong* yet irresistibly captivating. He had to follow it. He couldn't explain why, but he knew in his very bones that he had no choice.

He banked sharply to the left, veering away from the mountains that had always been his home, and began to glide over unfamiliar lands. Below him, the world seemed to unfurl in a never-ending stretch of rolling hills, ancient forests, and winding rivers that shimmered with strange, ethereal light. The air was thick with magic, the kind Longzi had never encountered before - magic that seemed to hum in the atmosphere, filling the air with a sweet, almost intoxicating scent. Every tree he passed seemed to glow with an otherworldly aura, and the streams that cut through the land sparkled with a strange, vibrant energy, as if they held secrets in their depths.

But even as the beauty of this strange new world enchanted him, the call kept growing stronger, reverberating through him like a drumbeat in the distance. It pulled him forward, faster and faster, until the landscape below him blurred, the world spinning into a wild rush of colour and sound.

Longzi's golden scales shimmered with the intensity of the magic all around him. It felt like power - raw and untamed. But it was not the warmth of the magic he had known. This magic was darker, more dangerous. It didn't feel like something to be shared, like the kind he had spread in Qingyun. No, this felt like something to be *taken* - something that sought to control.

The deeper he flew into the heart of the land, the stronger the magic became. The trees seemed to close in around him, their branches twisting into strange shapes, and the rivers, once so beautiful, now rippled with an eerie, unnatural current. The ground beneath him trembled slightly, as if the very earth was alive, watching, waiting.

And then, at the edge of a dark, shadowy forest, he saw it. A towering fortress, carved into the side of a jagged mountain, rose like a dark beacon against the sky. The structure seemed to pulse with an unnatural energy, its jagged spires twisting toward the sky like fingers stretching for the stars. It was *wrong*, something deep within Longzi's instincts told him, but the call was coming from within that fortress, its source undeniable.

Longzi hovered above the fortress, the wind whipping through his mane of golden scales. The magic in the air was thick now, pressing down on him, making it harder to breathe. He could feel the pull, stronger than ever, tugging at his heart.

Without thinking, he descended toward the fortress, the walls looming closer, the shadows growing darker. As he drew near, the call grew clearer, a whisper that slid beneath his thoughts, creeping into his very soul. But something in that whisper - a flicker of something cold, something familiar yet *wrong* - caused a pang of unease in Longzi's chest.

He reached the high gates of the fortress, and just as his claws scraped against the stone, the call ceased.

A chilling silence fell.

Longzi hovered in the air, wings beating softly, as the gates of the fortress slowly creaked open. What waited on the other side? Was it another dragon, as he had hoped, or was it something darker, something that had lured him here for its own reasons? The wind howled in the distance, and Longzi felt an icy chill run through him.

He had crossed into a land he did not understand, where the magic felt wrong, where the pull of the call was both irresistible and terrifying.

And yet, he could not turn back.

The gates opened fully, revealing the darkened courtyard beyond, and the cold, unnerving magic that called him forward.

With a deep breath, Longzi flew inside, unaware that his fate had already been sealed.

## CHAPTER EIGHT

# The Sorcerer's Trap

With a deep breath, Longzi steeled himself and entered the fortress.

The gates creaked open, as though they had not moved in centuries. Inside, the stone walls were cold to the touch, slick with moisture that clung to his claws. The darkened halls stretched endlessly, winding through the fortress like a labyrinth, each turn leading deeper into the heart of the sorcerer's domain.

At the very centre of the fortress, he found him.

*Sorcerer Zhen.*

The man who stood before Longzi seemed to radiate power, his long, silver hair flowing like a river of moonlight around his pale face. His eyes were a piercing shade of amber, cold and calculating, gleaming with a hunger that made Longzi's heart race. His robes were black, embroidered with intricate symbols that seemed to shift and writhe as though alive.

Zhen's smile was cold, almost predatory. 'I've been waiting for you, dragon,' he said in a voice that slithered through the air, smooth as silk yet laced with an unspoken threat.

Longzi took a step back instinctively, his claws scraping across the cold stone. His golden scales gleamed faintly in the dim light, but the magic in the air seemed to dull their brilliance, casting a shadow over his form.

'You-' Longzi began, his voice low and cautious. 'You're the one who called me here. What do you want?'

Zhen's lips curled into a slow smile. 'What do I want, you ask?' He chuckled, the sound echoing off the stone walls like the rattle of chains. 'I want power. I want control over the greatest force the world has ever known.' His gaze flicked to Longzi's golden scales, a look of almost reverence in his eyes. 'I want you, dragon.'

Longzi's eyes narrowed. 'I will never be controlled by anyone. Not by you, and not by any sorcerer.' His wings unfurled, a flash of gold cutting through the darkness of the room.

Zhen's smile only widened, and with a subtle flick of his fingers, a burst of energy shot through the air. Before Longzi could react, the magic slammed into him, sending a wave of searing cold through his body. The dragon's wings faltered, his claws scraping against the stone as he struggled to remain upright.

'That's where you're wrong, dragon,' Zhen said, his voice now laced with power. 'You see, I've spent years studying the magic of your kind, and I've learned how to control it. How to control *you*.'

Longzi's golden scales shimmered and flickered, but the magic surrounding him twisted, suppressing the warmth and light he carried within. His muscles locked in place, and he felt a powerful pressure build within him - a spell stronger than anything he had ever encountered before.

'No…' Longzi grunted, trying to summon his magic, but the more he struggled, the more tightly the spell gripped him. His wings, once free and strong, drooped helplessly at his sides. He could feel his strength slipping away, like a flame slowly being snuffed out.

Zhen stepped forward, his cold amber eyes gleaming with triumph. 'You are mine now, dragon. And your power will be mine to command.' With another gesture, the sorcerer's magic coiled around Longzi like a tightening noose. The dragon's magic, once bright and radiant, began to grow dim, locked away deep inside him.

Longzi's heart pounded in his chest, fear and anger swirling within him. He tried again to free himself, to break the sorcerer's hold, but the magic kept him immobile. His wings, his claws, even his thoughts - all felt sluggish, heavy, and bound by invisible chains.

The warmth of his golden scales faded, replaced by the cold, oppressive grip of Zhen's dark spell.

'You will serve me, dragon,' Zhen continued, his voice a mere whisper in the vast, echoing hall. 'Your power will conquer kingdoms. Your roar will bring nations to their knees. And when you are mine, nothing will stand in my way.'

Longzi's heart sank. He had been free, so free, to soar the skies, to protect the lands he loved. And now, here, in this forsaken place, he was nothing more than a prisoner.

But even as the darkness closed in around him, he refused to give up. He could feel the faintest flicker of his magic, buried deep beneath the sorcerer's control. It was weak, far weaker than it had ever been, but it was still there. Longzi would fight. He would *never* submit to Zhen's cruelty. No matter how tight the sorcerer's magic became, he would not allow it to snuff out the light within him.

But for now, he could do nothing.

Longzi was trapped.

## CHAPTER NINE

# The Darkening of Longzi

The air in Sorcerer Zhen's fortress was thick and oppressive, laden with an unnatural chill that seemed to seep into Longzi's very bones. The once-glorious dragon, whose golden scales had shimmered like the sun, now lay coiled on the cold, stone floor of the chamber, his massive form shackled by chains of dark, enchanted iron that held him in place. The flickering flames in the hearth cast long, twisting shadows on the walls, dancing like spectres, and the air reeked of magic so dark and cold that it made Longzi's heart ache with a feeling he had never known before.

The golden dragon's once-glowing scales had begun to fade, losing their lustre with each passing day. They had started to turn a dull bronze, and now they were beginning to shift, slowly darkening, the familiar warmth of his magic replaced with a hollow coldness that clawed at his very soul. The change was subtle at first, a slight twinge of discomfort when he tried to summon his power, a faint tightening in his chest when he attempted to soar through the skies. But as the days bled into weeks, the transformation grew more pronounced.

His once brilliant, shimmering coat was now ashen, and the gleam of his eyes had dulled into a stormy, murky hue, clouded by something far darker. Longzi could feel the magic inside him, the power that had once been a source of joy and light, now twisting and warping, like a flame that had been smothered by an unrelenting wind. His breath, once warm and rich, now sent out icy gusts into the air. Each exhale felt like a crackling ember of power slipping further from his reach, and there was nothing he could do to stop it.

The chains that bound him were more than physical. They were magical, forged from the most potent dark enchantments Sorcerer

Zhen had woven into his very being. Every time Longzi attempted to break free, the chains tightened, sending waves of numbing magic through his body, dulling his senses, and leaving him feeling weak and helpless. He could barely remember the days when he had flown freely through the skies, feeling the rush of wind beneath his wings, the sense of freedom and strength that had once defined him. Now, all that was left was the suffocating weight of Zhen's power.

Sorcerer Zhen would often visit him in the dead of night, his amber eyes gleaming with satisfaction, his lips curled into a cruel smile. 'You will learn, dragon,' Zhen would whisper, his voice like a serpent's hiss. 'Power is not given, it is *taken*. And I will make you understand that the true strength lies in domination, not freedom.'

Longzi could do nothing but listen, his heart burning with frustration, but unable to summon the courage or the power to defy the sorcerer's will.

Then came the first mission. Zhen had ordered Longzi to fly, to spread fear and terror across the villages near the fortress. At first, Longzi resisted - his heart still held the flickers of kindness from Qingyun, the place where he had once known peace. But the sorcerer's spells gripped him tight, and his once-joyful roar had become an unnatural, bone-rattling sound that echoed through the valleys, sending the people fleeing in terror.

With every village Longzi decimated, his scales grew darker, his power more twisted. It felt as though every fire he ignited, every house he destroyed, was not just the work of his claws, but the extension of Zhen's cruel will, feeding the sorcerer's dark magic. The dragon's once pure heart began to crack, piece by piece, until all that was left was an empty, hollow shell, driven by bitterness and rage.

He had once brought life to the land. Now, he brought death.

Longzi's magic, once the lifeblood of the world, was now turned against it. It poured out of him in waves of destructive energy, the ground shaking with every beat of his wings. Villages that had once flourished under his protection were left in ruins, the skies darkened with smoke, and the air filled with the scent of ash and despair. His roar, once full of laughter and joy, now struck terror into the hearts of those who heard it. His once-golden scales, now a dull, angry black, flickered with bursts of corrupted power, sparking with energy that did not belong in him.

Every day, the dragon's descent continued, and the sorcerer's grip tightened. Zhen watched with growing satisfaction as the land quivered beneath the weight of Longzi's destructive power. The sorcerer had long dreamed of this moment - of bending a dragon's magic to his will. Now, Longzi was nothing more than a tool, a weapon to further Zhen's dominion over the land.

'Once I have you under my command,' Zhen had said one night, standing before Longzi's chained form, 'I will bring the entire world to its knees. And you will be the one to break them.'

Longzi wanted to fight. He wanted to scream, to roar, to break free of the chains that held him, to flee into the skies once more and feel the wind beneath his wings. But he could feel it - the bitter cold of Zhen's magic, eating away at his very soul. The more he gave in to the sorcerer's commands, the less of the dragon he recognized in himself. The golden light that had once burned so brightly within him had all but extinguished. All that remained was a shadow of what he had been, a twisted echo of the dragon that had once been full of hope.

And yet, even amidst the darkness that now consumed him, something lingered. A faint whisper at the edges of his mind. A memory. A time when he had been kind, when he had known peace, when his heart had been whole.

But it was slipping away. Slowly. Relentlessly.

The darkness was all-encompassing now, a force that seemed to devour everything in its path.

Longzi had become a monster.

And there was nothing he could do to stop it.

# CHAPTER TEN

# The Sorcerer's Conquests

The land had become a shadow of itself.

Where once there had been lush forests, vibrant meadows, and peaceful villages, there was only ruin. The earth, once rich with life, now lay scarred and barren, the soil cracked and dry, as though the land itself mourned its loss. The air was thick with the scent of ash, and the sun barely seemed to shine through the ever-present clouds of smoke that swirled above the wreckage. Blackened fields stretched out across the landscape, where crops had been burned to the ground, and the ruins of homes sat like empty shells, hollow and silent.

And above it all, the dragon flew.

Longzi, the once-golden dragon of Qingyun, now soared through the darkened skies, his wings cutting through the air with unnatural force. His scales, which had once gleamed like the finest gold, had turned an obsidian black, the dark colour spreading like ink across the expanse of his mighty form. The sharp, jagged points of his tail and wings now seemed more like weapons than parts of a creature once full of life and warmth. His eyes, once bright with curiosity and joy, were now empty, cold, and distant - void of the kindness that had once filled them.

Behind him, the ever-watchful Sorcerer Zhen rode high on a platform of floating dark stone, his hands raised to the heavens, a triumphant grin stretching across his pale face. The sorcerer's amber eyes gleamed with feverish excitement as he watched the dragon wreak havoc on the land, each village they destroyed feeding into his growing power, each conquest bringing him closer to his ultimate goal.

Together, they were unstoppable.

Longzi's roar echoed through the valley, a sound that once filled the world with wonder, now only bringing terror. It was a roar that shook the earth beneath their feet, a call to arms that was both a warning and a declaration of destruction. Villagers cowered in fear, knowing that if they did not flee in time, their homes would be levelled, their families scattered in the wake of the dragon's fury.

The first village they conquered had been the quiet farming community of Tianshi. Longzi had torn through the fields and the homes, his once-gentle breath now a torrent of fire that reduced everything to ashes. The villagers had tried to fight, their hands trembling with weapons too small to face the might of a dragon, but it had been futile. Longzi's flames had razed the town to the ground, the village elders left weeping as their people fled into the wilderness, knowing they could not hope to stand against the dragon's wrath.

And so it had gone, village after village. Each one fell before them, each one crushed under the weight of Longzi's fire and Zhen's unyielding will. They were a force of nature now, a dark storm that swept across the kingdom, leaving only desolation in their wake.

With each victory, Longzi's transformation deepened. The golden glow that had once defined him seemed to fade more and more, until his scales reflected no light at all. The magic that had once coursed through him in bright, warm waves now flowed cold and jagged, twisting in unnatural ways, feeding the dark power that Zhen had over him. The dragon's power was no longer his own; it belonged to the sorcerer, bound tightly by chains of magic that drained Longzi's will.

But Zhen's power grew stronger with every conquest. The people who once sang songs of Longzi's greatness now whispered of his fall from grace, speaking of him in fearful tones, as though he were a creature of nightmare rather than the dragon of legend.

And Zhen revelled in it.

'Do you see, dragon?' Zhen's voice, smooth and silken, always found its way to Longzi's ears, no matter how far apart they were.

'With each village you lay to waste, my power grows. Soon, I will have all the kingdoms under my command. They will bow to me as their true king, and you will be the instrument of their destruction.'

Longzi said nothing. His wings beat the air with mechanical precision, each stroke filled with a sense of obligation rather than choice. He could feel his power, his magic, stretching thin with every turn of the earth, his once-bright spirit slipping further away. But still, he did not fight. The chains that held him bound so tightly, both magical and physical, seemed too strong to break.

Zhen had been right: power was not something that could be given freely. It was something that could only be taken - and Longzi had learned, all too well, that he was nothing but a pawn in the sorcerer's game.

One night, after another village had fallen to their wrath, Zhen stood at the pinnacle of a blackened tower, overlooking the destruction they had wrought. His hands were raised high, his eyes gleaming with madness.

'We will not stop here, dragon,' Zhen declared to the night air, his voice filled with conviction. 'I will bring the kingdoms of this land to their knees. Every king, every ruler will bow before me. And you, my obedient dragon, will help me achieve it. We will spread across the world, our shadows covering every corner of this land. We will build an empire of darkness, and no one will be able to stand in our way.'

The air crackled with power as Zhen's magic surged around him, dark tendrils of energy swirling and twisting like serpents. Longzi, trapped in his bonds, watched from the shadows, his obsidian scales gleaming faintly in the dim light. There was no joy in the sight, no warmth in the way his magic responded to Zhen's call. Instead, there was only emptiness, the slow-burning realization that there was nothing left for him in this dark path.

Zhen's eyes flicked to the dragon, a smirk tugging at the corners of his lips. 'Do not think you are free of this, Longzi. Your magic belongs to me now. And soon, the world will belong to us.'

MARK A. BROWN

As the sorcerer spoke, Longzi's heart pulsed with a faint memory - a memory of a golden sky, a village where people once smiled and greeted him with love, the warmth of the bond he had shared with Li Wei.

But it was only a memory. A distant memory.

And it was slipping further away with every passing day.

## CHAPTER ELEVEN

# The Return to Qingyun

The village of Qingyun had changed little in the time since Longzi's departure. The rice fields stretched out in neat rows, golden grains swaying in the breeze, and the orchards stood heavy with ripe fruit, their branches drooping with the weight of nature's bounty. The scent of jasmine and plum blossoms still carried through the air, a sweet, comforting fragrance that had always marked the changing of seasons in this peaceful place.

Li Wei stood at the edge of the village, watching the sun dip behind the mountains, painting the sky in hues of pink and orange. His heart, though full of quiet pride in his village, had become something more in the years since Longzi's flight. The magic that the dragon had gifted him had grown stronger, more refined. It pulsed within him like a second heartbeat, a steady rhythm that seemed to align with the land itself. He could sense the life around him - the deep-rooted pulse of the earth, the gentle sway of the trees, the flow of the river. It was all part of him now.

But today, something was different.

The air had changed.

A chill had settled over the village, creeping in from the north, stealing the warmth of the evening. Li Wei's hand instinctively tightened around the talisman Longzi had once given him - a smooth, golden scale from the dragon's chest. It was warm to the touch, though the warmth felt distant, like a fading memory.

He felt it before he saw it - the faint hum in the air, the sudden shift in the balance of magic. It was no longer the vibrant, life-affirming magic that Longzi had once brought to Qingyun. No, this felt colder. Darker. A distortion of the very magic that had once made the village thrive.

A low rumble echoed across the sky, and Li Wei's eyes narrowed. His senses were sharp, attuned to the land, but this… this was different. The magic was wrong, twisted, and he could feel it coming from the direction of the mountains.

The wind picked up, howling through the trees, carrying with it a terrible foreboding. Dark clouds rolled across the horizon, blotting out the light of the sun as though a great shadow were descending upon the village. The storm did not look natural - it felt like a living thing, spreading its darkness across the land. It wasn't just a storm, it was an omen.

Li Wei's heart skipped a beat. He knew what this meant.

Longzi was coming.

But it wasn't the joyful, golden dragon who had once soared through these skies. No, this presence was cold - corrupted. The magic he felt was no longer filled with the warmth of life. It was heavy, oppressive, and angry. It gnawed at the edges of his mind, as if trying to push its way into his thoughts, trying to take over.

'No,' Li Wei whispered to himself. His throat tightened. *It can't be him.* Longzi could not have fallen so far. The dragon, his friend, the one who had once brought prosperity and peace to the village, could not have become this dark force.

But deep within, Li Wei felt the truth. The magic had changed, and it had come from Longzi. The bond they had shared was still there, but now it was tainted by something that had once been foreign to the dragon - a sense of malice, of destruction. Longzi's golden heart had been replaced by something darker, twisted.

Li Wei swallowed hard, stepping back from the edge of the village square. His mind raced. He was no longer a child, no longer the dreamer who had once found joy in the simplest things. The magic Longzi had given him had changed him, too. It had given him strength, not just to protect the village, but to stand against whatever dark force had corrupted his oldest friend.

The first drops of rain began to fall, cold and heavy, as the storm finally broke over the village. The wind picked up, whipping the trees in violent gusts. In the distance, a flash of lightning illuminated the sky, and for a moment, Li Wei saw it - an immense shadow, larger than any bird, circling above the mountains. He didn't need to see its shape to know who it was.

*Longzi.*

But this was not the dragon he had once known. This was something else. Something that filled Li Wei's chest with a cold ache.

He ran.

Through the village, past the rice fields, and toward the hills, where the wind howled louder and louder. He could feel the magic swirling around him, but it was different now - faint and distant, as though a connection he had once relied on was slipping through his fingers like water.

When he reached the top of the hill, Li Wei stopped and stood, watching the horizon. The storm darkened the world around him, but he did not flinch. He had faced dangers before - wild animals, fierce storms - but none of them had felt like this. None of them had made his heart ache in the way this storm did, this presence. He could feel the bond between him and Longzi, but it was strained, stretched thin, like a rope pulled too tight.

*I have to save him.* The thought echoed through Li Wei's mind, fierce and clear.

A shadow passed across the sky - vast, enormous. It circled above the mountains, moving toward him. For a moment, Li Wei thought he saw the faintest gleam of gold in the clouds, but it was swallowed by the darkness that followed.

*No...* Li Wei's voice was barely a whisper.

Longzi was coming.

But this time, he was not coming to bring magic, to bring joy. This time, he was coming to bring destruction. And Li Wei could feel it, his old friend, the dragon he had known, was lost to the darkness.

The storm raged around him, and in the distance, the darkened silhouette of Longzi flew ever closer, his presence a cold, twisted reminder of the friendship Li Wei had fought so hard to protect.

But now, the dragon was a prisoner - held captive by a sorcerer's cruel magic. And it was up to Li Wei to save him.

## CHAPTER TWELVE

# The Battle for Qingyun

The storm had turned the sky a brooding shade of grey, and the air crackled with an unnatural energy. It was as though the land itself was holding its breath, waiting for the inevitable. The villagers of Qingyun had gathered in the square, looking nervously toward the darkened horizon. The once peaceful land now pulsed with a sense of dread. The gentle winds that had once carried the scent of blossoms now howled like wolves, biting at their skin and whipping the trees into violent convulsions.

Li Wei stood at the centre of the village, his heart pounding in his chest, his hands clasped tightly around the golden scale Longzi had given him. It pulsed with magic, though the warmth it had once held now felt faint and distant. The bond between them, the magic that had once connected them so deeply, was now strained, tainted by the dark forces that had taken hold of the dragon.

Above, the storm clouds parted for a moment, and the first terrible sound echoed across the valley. A roar so deep and powerful it shook the ground beneath their feet. It was a sound that sent a shiver through Li Wei's bones, a cry of pain, rage, and something far darker.

There, descending from the heavens, was Longzi - his once-golden scales now twisted into black, obsidian-like armour, his wings blotting out the sky. The dragon was no longer the playful, golden creature that had once filled Qingyun with light, he was a shadow of his former self, his presence a living nightmare.

Beside him floated Sorcerer Zhen, his cold eyes glinting with malice as he surveyed the village below. The sorcerer's dark robes billowed in the wind, and his staff crackled with dark magic. He laughed softly, a low, menacing sound that reverberated in the hearts of the villagers.

'Do you see now, little village?' Zhen's voice boomed. 'Your protector has become your destroyer. I have bound this mighty creature to my will. There is nothing you can do. No one can stand against me.'

The villagers quailed, fear seeping into their hearts, but Li Wei stood tall. He could feel the weight of his responsibility, the power that still lingered within him from the magic Longzi had given him. He could sense the dragon's presence within the storm - his sadness, his confusion, and his fury. But beneath it all, Li Wei could feel the faintest flicker of the dragon he had known, the bond they had shared, still alive.

'No,' Li Wei whispered to himself, taking a deep breath. 'I won't give up on you, Longzi.'

Stepping forward, Li Wei raised his hand, the magic within him thrumming like a second heartbeat. The villagers looked to him, uncertain but hopeful. In the face of this terror, Li Wei was their only hope. His connection to Longzi was their only chance.

Sorcerer Zhen's eyes narrowed as Li Wei stood before him, his arms raised in defiance. 'You truly believe you can stop me, child?' the sorcerer sneered. 'This dragon is mine. He will destroy you all.'

Li Wei's heart hammered in his chest, but he did not waver. He could feel the dragon's magic deep within him - the gift Longzi had given him - but it felt faint. It wasn't enough. The sorcerer's dark influence was too strong. The storm around them grew even fiercer, crackling with Zhen's power, and Li Wei's knees nearly buckled under the weight of the magic pressing down on him.

But then, as he stood there, something changed.

A memory flickered in his mind - the first time Longzi had flown around Qingyun, the joy they had shared, the laughter that had filled the air. The connection they had, so pure, so full of trust.

# THE DRAGON'S EGG

*The bond between us is not just magic. It's friendship. It's love. And that will always be stronger than darkness.*

With that thought, Li Wei closed his eyes and focused on the heart of the magic - the warmth, the kindness, the joy that Longzi had always brought to the village. He reached into that memory, into that connection, and he called out to his friend.

'Longzi!' he cried, his voice ringing out over the storm. 'I know you're still in there. Remember who you are! Remember the magic we shared. You are not his to control! You are free! *You are my friend!*'

For a long moment, there was silence, save for the howling wind. Then, the dragon's massive form paused in midair. His eyes, once cold and dark, flickered with a glimmer of recognition.

The storm seemed to pause, as if the very earth was holding its breath. Then, with a deep, thunderous roar, Longzi shook his massive head. The blackened scales covering his body began to shimmer, a faint glint of gold breaking through the darkness. His wings stretched wide, and with a cry of pain, the dragon fought against the sorcerer's control.

Li Wei's heart soared. He could feel it - the warmth returning, the bond rekindling, the magic awakening.

'No!' Zhen screamed, his voice filled with fury. His hand shot out, casting dark tendrils of magic toward the dragon, but Longzi's magic surged forward, breaking through the sorcerer's grasp.

With a mighty roar, Longzi's scales burst into golden brilliance, and the dragon's true form was revealed once more. The magic that had been twisted by Zhen's dark spell now exploded outward in a brilliant wave of light, shattering the sorcerer's dark magic and sending him reeling.

Li Wei stood firm as the dragon's light illuminated the entire village. The storm dissipated, and the dark clouds began to break apart, revealing a clear sky above. Longzi's roar was one of power - but it was also one of freedom.

Sorcerer Zhen staggered, his hands raised in a futile attempt to summon more dark magic, but it was no use. The magic that had once given him power was now shattered, defeated by the force of Longzi's will.

With a final, defiant cry, Longzi turned his gaze upon Zhen, and in a burst of pure, radiant magic, the sorcerer was struck down, his dark powers unravelling before the might of the freed dragon.

As the dust settled and the storm cleared, Longzi hovered above Qingyun, his golden scales shimmering in the soft light of the returning sun. The villagers, stunned and silent, watched as the dragon turned toward Li Wei, his eyes filled with warmth and gratitude.

Li Wei smiled, his heart light with relief and joy. 'You're free,' he said, his voice soft but filled with certainty. 'Welcome home, Longzi.'

And as the dragon descended slowly to the ground, the bond between them - stronger than ever - was clear to all who witnessed it. Longzi was not just a creature of magic. He was a friend, a protector, a symbol of the hope that had always burned within the heart of Qingyun.

Together, they had saved the village - and together, they would ensure its magic would never fade.

## CHAPTER THIRTEEN

# A New Dawn

The village of Qingyun had never looked more beautiful. The dawn broke over the horizon, painting the sky in hues of gold and amber, as if the sun itself had been reborn along with the village. The orchards, once heavy with the shadows of fear, were now bursting with fruit, their branches laden with the ripest peaches and apples. The rice fields, nourished by the magic of Longzi and Li Wei, stretched out like green carpets, undulating in the morning breeze. It was a sight of pure, unblemished peace - one that Li Wei had once only dreamed of, but now stood before him in living colour.

The air was warm, fragrant with the scent of blooming flowers, and the gentle song of birds filled the quiet morning. Qingyun had returned to the simple, tranquil life it had known before darkness had ever threatened to consume it. The villagers went about their tasks, their hearts light, their spirits high. The magic of the land was vibrant once more, and its keeper was no longer a prisoner of dark forces, but free to roam the skies.

Li Wei stood atop the hill that overlooked the village, his eyes watching the golden rays of the sun stretch across the land. His heart was full of gratitude and peace, but there was a sadness, too. Longzi had come to him as a friend, a protector, and had shown him the true power of magic - magic born of kindness, trust, and friendship. But now, the time had come for the dragon to continue his journey, to spread the magic that had once filled Qingyun far and wide.

The dragon was ready.

From the horizon, a shimmering streak of gold appeared in the sky - Longzi's wings cutting through the air, his golden scales gleaming like a star that had broken free of the night. He soared higher and higher, the sun lighting his form as he approached Li Wei. The bond between them was palpable, even from this distance, a connection that was stronger than any words could express.

As Longzi landed softly before Li Wei, the ground seemed to hum beneath their feet, as if the earth itself was acknowledging their bond. The dragon lowered his head, his eyes bright with affection and warmth, and Li Wei stepped forward, his heart swelling with emotion.

'I will always remember you, Li Wei,' Longzi said, his voice soft and filled with deep meaning. 'I am proud of you. The village is in safe hands. The magic of this place lives in you now, as it always has.'

Li Wei smiled, though his eyes glistened with unshed tears. 'I will guard it with everything I have, Longzi. And I will never forget the lessons you've taught me - the power of kindness, of loyalty, of the magic that lives in a pure heart.'

Longzi's wings fluttered gently, and he looked out over the village one last time. The golden light of the sun reflected off his shimmering scales, making him appear almost otherworldly, a creature of legend.

'I must continue my journey, my friend,' Longzi said, his voice low but steady. 'There are places beyond these mountains that need magic, places where hope has dimmed. The world is vast, and there is much to be done. But know this, Li Wei, as long as I fly, as long as I breathe, the magic I shared with you will always be with you. And I will carry a part of Qingyun in my heart, always.'

Li Wei nodded, though his chest tightened with the knowledge that this was a true farewell. But deep within him, he knew that Longzi's magic would never truly leave him. It would live on in the very air of the village, in the roots of the trees, in the blooming of every flower, and in the hearts of those who believed in the goodness of the world.

'I'll be here,' Li Wei said softly. 'And if you ever need me, I'll always be ready. Our bond is unbreakable.'

With that, Longzi raised his wings, casting one last glance at the village he had saved, the village that had given him a place to call home. With a powerful flap of his wings, the dragon lifted off into the sky, soaring higher and higher until he became a speck in the distance, a streak of gold against the vast expanse of blue.

Li Wei stood there for a long time, watching the sky, feeling the lingering warmth of the magic that had always surrounded them both. The wind shifted gently, carrying the whispers of the past with it.

He knew that Longzi's adventures would take him to many places, and that the magic he spread would light up even the darkest corners of the world. But Li Wei also knew that his work, too, was far from over. The bond between them remained, a bond that would never fade, no matter how far the dragon flew.

He turned back toward the village, his heart full of love for the people who had become his family and for the land that had been so kind to him. The fields stretched before him, rich with the promise of a prosperous future. And in that moment, Li Wei felt that his journey had only just begun.

With the gift of magic in his hands and the protection of the dragon in his heart, he would guard Qingyun with all the courage and kindness he could muster. He would nurture the magic that had flowed through Longzi and, in doing so, he would ensure that it would never fade. The world might be vast, but here, in this place of hope and harmony, magic would always live.

Li Wei smiled as the morning sun bathed the village in its golden light. A new dawn had arrived.

And with it, a new beginning.

# Epilogue

Years passed in the village of Qingyun, and time, as it always does, carried on like the steady flow of a river. But though the seasons changed, and the years wove their quiet tapestry across the land, the magic that Longzi had brought with him remained, woven deep into the very fabric of the village. It thrived in the green fields that rippled like a sea, in the orchards that bloomed with fruit year after year, and in the hearts of the people who had learned to cherish kindness and loyalty above all else.

Li Wei had grown into a young man, his hair now touched with streaks of silver, though his eyes still carried the bright, hopeful spark of the boy he had once been. He had become not only a protector of the village but a wise leader, whose counsel was sought by villagers far and wide. He knew the land like the back of his hand, and the magic that Longzi had gifted him flowed through him as naturally as the rivers that ran through the valley.

But most of all, Li Wei had become the keeper of the dragon's legacy.

Every year, as the first light of dawn touched the peaks of the great mountains, Li Wei would stand atop the same hill where he had last seen his friend soar into the sky. There, he would wait, watching for a glimmer of gold in the sky, the faintest shimmer of Longzi's wings.

And though the dragon never returned to Qingyun in body, Li Wei could feel him in the air - the magic that had once been twisted and dark was now a part of the world once more. Wherever there was kindness, wherever there was love, Longzi's spirit lingered.

One evening, as the sun set behind the mountains, painting the sky in shades of purple and gold, Li Wei stood alone on the hill, his hands resting gently on the railing of the wooden fence. The wind carried the scent of jasmine and honeysuckle, and he closed his eyes, remembering Longzi. He thought of their journey, the magic they had shared, and the bond that had saved the world.

A soft rustling of wings broke the quiet, and for a moment, Li Wei thought he imagined it. But then, a flicker of light caught his eye.

Far above, on the edge of the horizon, Longzi appeared - a brilliant streak of gold that shone brighter than any star. His wings, wide and powerful, caught the evening light, and he soared in a circle high above the village, just as he had done in the days when they had been together.

Li Wei smiled, his heart full. Longzi didn't need to return to stay. His journey would never end, for magic was not bound by time or place. The dragon had shared his gift, and now, that gift was alive in every leaf, every grain of rice, every bloom of a flower in Qingyun. Magic was in the heart of the village and in the hearts of the people who had learned to love it.

As the dragon disappeared into the distance, Li Wei whispered softly to the wind, 'Thank you, my friend. You'll never be forgotten.'

And as he turned back toward the village, Li Wei knew that the world was vast, full of wonders yet to be discovered. Longzi would continue to spread his magic wherever it was needed, just as Li Wei would protect the village with the strength of his heart, the strength of their bond.

In the distance, the village of Qingyun stood - a place of peace, of magic, and of memories.

And though Longzi's wings no longer beat above the village, the magic that had changed their world would always remain, a legacy of hope that lived on for generations to come.

Printed in Great Britain
by Amazon